The Somme Rat

The Somme Rat

Copyright © 2023 Bob Stone

All rights reserved.

One

Alfred Sweeney hadn't expected to spend the last day of July like this. July was the time of year when it started to get warm and summer really began. April could be damp and some of that rain lingered on into May, giving way to better weather, but even June was still uncertain sometimes. You knew where you were with July. That was when the sky got bluer and the girls got prettier and the days felt like they could go on forever. A year ago, he had sat with Daisy Atwell, with their backs against the village cross and she hadn't minded when he reached out and took her hand. She hadn't looked at him, but smiled the sort of smile you do when you're thinking something private and entwined her fingers around his. Later, before they went home, she had let him kiss her, just once and she kept her lips closed, but there was promise in it of more to come if he played his cards right. When he left, she promised to wait for him and to write to him, but she never came to the station to see him off. She said she didn't want to say goodbye because it sounded final. She didn't write and he didn't expect her to. It had been one of those things that start in July and seem like a fine idea, but don't make it through the winter to spring, like the flowers in the beds around the village cross. This year, the girls would have to talk to each other, because all the lads had gone.

Now Alfie Sweeney was on his own. His legs were covered in so much mud that it felt like they'd set solid and would never move again. They were covered in other things, too, but he tried not to think about that. There was blood, his own and that of some of the other lads, and the stuff that came out of Jimmy Clayton's head when it exploded right next to him. If he thought of that, he'd have to think about the look on what was left of Jimmy's face when it hit his leg as he fell. He had scrabbled for Alfie with what remained of his strength, trying to grab hold of Alfie's belt, but Alfie had to kick out at his best friend so he wouldn't be dragged down into the mud with him. He'd had to leave Jimmy to sink but didn't have time to worry about it. Jimmy was as good as dead before he hit the sodden ground, and there was a wave of other lads coming up behind Alfie so he had to keep moving. If you stopped, you got trampled and ended up like Jimmy without even being shot. At least the dead didn't drown, and it was drowning in the mud that Alfie feared most. If you got a bullet to the head or hit by a grenade, you probably wouldn't know much about it. If you fell, you would sink slowly, the filthy, insect-ridden slime filling your mouth and nose until you couldn't breathe any more and the ground swallowed you up. So he had left his best friend where he was and forced his legs to move him onwards. He didn't get far.

They had only pressed on a hundred yards or so, when a shell exploded in front of him, blowing a crater in the ground and sending a cascade showering down. Alfie felt hot mud plaster his face, and, blinded by that and the dense smoke that filled the air, tried to swerve to his left to avoid the shell crater and ran straight into a coil of barbed wire. At first, because he couldn't see, he didn't know what had happened; all he knew was that he couldn't move. Something had grabbed his arms and legs and wouldn't let him go any further. It was only when the razor-sharp barbs tore through his uniform jacket and trousers and into the flesh of his arms and thighs that he understood. He blinked frantically, trying to clear the mud and debris from his eyes, and was about to shake his head, when, through the grey film he could make out a strand of the wire right in front of his face. Had he stopped another inch further on, it would have had his eyes. Before he could think any more about his situation, a further hail of gunfire churned up the mire at his feet and one bullet shattered his left kneecap. He blacked out and hung on the barbed wire like a pile of discarded rags, while all around him the air burned and men screamed.

Two

Alfie hung on the barbed wire and dreamed he was back in the village. It was late winter, but one of those winter days when the rain goes off and the sun breaks through, promising that spring was just around the corner. Everywhere smelled fresh and clean and after its dousing, the grass looked just that bit greener. Alfie had been working in the field, trying to do what he could before the rain turned the soil to mush, but was now leaning against a gate, having a smoke and drying off in the sun. Up the lane, he could see Jimmy Clayton walking hand in hand with his sweetheart, Mary. Everyone knew that Jimmy and Mary were to be wed soon, but this war had cast a shadow over everything. Some point soon, Alfie would have to leave the fields to his dad to sort out, and he wasn't the man he used to be any more. God only knew what kind of a mess Alfie would be coming back to. He had tossed the idea of signing up backwards and forwards for weeks. He knew from what the old ones who read the papers said that the war needed fighting, and that the King wanted every man to play his part, and he knew deep down that it was the right thing to do. But his ma had a lot on her hands with his little brother and the baby too, and his dad couldn't do much without being near bent double with pain. If Alfie wasn't here to work the land, then the farm could go bust. He was torn between his King and his family and didn't know what to do.

Jimmy gave Mary a hug and a kiss and watched her walk away, then came sauntering up the lane to the gate. Alfie flicked the stub of his cigarette away and took the packet out of his pocket. He offered one to Jimmy and took another for himself. He lit them both and they smoked for a minute. They'd known each other since they got put together at the village school and didn't always need words, but Alfie could tell his friend was troubled about something.

"Mary all right?" he asked.

"She's a cracker that girl. Just wish sometimes she'd shut up about getting wed. Says vicar will do it quick if I'm going to sign up. I said everyone'll think I've knocked her up."

"It's only a matter of time the way you two go at it."

"Don't talk like that about her," Jimmy said, but smiled. "She's a good girl, is Mary."

"Then maybe you should marry her."

"Maybe. She said if I was going off to Christ knows where, she'd rather I left a wife behind. I said, what if I end up leaving a widow?"

"What did she say to that?"

"She cried."

"I'm not bloody surprised. Anyhow, you'll come back a bloody hero, knowing you."

"You decided what to do?"

"Probably going. I think it's right."

Jimmy nodded and finished his cigarette.

"Hey, have you heard about the Pals?" he said.

"What?"

"It's this new thing. Seems you can sign up with a load of your mates and all go together. I heard there's a bunch of lads going from Chorley and someone said Accrington is sending loads. They want to get a gang from round here. George said he's up for it, and Arthur. And that lad who works at Howarth's farm, what's his name?"

"William something, I think. Croasdale. Something like that."

"So I was thinking. If we sign up with them, we'll all be going together. Better that than going on your own. What do you reckon?"

"I reckon it's a bloody trick," Alfie said. "They want lads out there so they've come up with this to make loads of them go at the same time."

"We're probably going to be sent out there anyroad, sooner or later. Better to go like this with lads you know, than get sent off to fight with strangers. Come on, Alfie lad, it makes sense."

"I'll think about it," Alfie said. "And I reckon *you* should think about making that girl of yours into Mrs. Clayton before you do."

"I don't think she'll give me much choice," Jimmy said. He laughed but it sounded hollow. "What about your Daisy?"

"She's not my Daisy. She's not anyone's Daisy that one. She'll not notice if I go or if I don't."

"Well think about that Pals thing. They'll be going before too long. You don't want to miss out."

Now Jimmy was in the mud and Mary was a widow because they ended up getting wed after all. George had fallen a couple of days ago, and Arthur had his leg blown off. No one knew what happened to the Croasdale lad. And Alfie was hanging on the barbed wire like a load of washing and there was a rat inspecting the blood that was flowing freely from his shattered kneecap and running over his boot.

Three

"You don't want people to think you're a coward," Daisy said.

In his mind's eye, Alfie was lying on his back in a field back home, not strung up on a field in France. All he could see was blue sky and small clouds. It was a warm spring day, warm enough for the grass to be dry enough to lie on, though Daisy had still insisted on bringing a blanket. Alfie was lying on the grass and Daisy was sitting on the blanket, plucking meadow flowers and running her hands through the clover looking for one with four leaves.

"Do I like butter?" she asked.

"Course you do. Everyone likes butter."

"No, Alfie. Look at me. Do I like butter?"

Alfie turned his head to look at her. She had her head tilted one side and was holding a buttercup under her chin. The flower cast a golden reflection under her chin and her eyes were the colour of cornflowers.

"Yes you like butter," he said. "You like butter a lot."

"I don't think I'd want to like it a lot," Daisy pouted. "If you eat too much, it makes you fat and I don't want to look like Peggy Barker. I don't look like Peggy Barker, do I, Alfie?"

"No, you don't." And she didn't. Daisy was pretty and petite and neither of those things applied to poor Peggy Barker. Nobody would be sitting in a field with Peggy, hoping she would shut up soon and do some more kissing. It wasn't often Alfie got the chance to be alone with Daisy and do any kissing. He wasn't sure if he was any good at it but did enjoy how it felt. Daisy wouldn't do any more than kiss yet, but he had hopes. They were by dashed Daisy's next question.

"Are you going to join the Pals?"

"I don't know. I think so. Do you think I should?"

"Well that's up to you. I can't tell you what to do, Alfie Sweeney. I think you'd look very handsome in the uniform though."

"Do you want me to go away and fight? I don't know when I'd be back. Would you wait for me?"

"Everyone else is going," Daisy said, evading the question. And then she said the words that would stay with him for a long time to come. "You don't want people to think you're a coward."

Alfie would never forget how he felt when she said that. It didn't really matter to him what anyone else thought of him. But it sounded very much as though Daisy meant herself. She would think he was a coward.

"I'm not a coward," he said, turning away from her.

"Well then. You could go there and come back a hero. You won't just be a farmhand anymore. You'll be a war hero."

"Would you marry me if I came back a hero?"

"Well I couldn't marry a coward. I might think about marrying a hero, though."

She leaned over then, and brushed her lips tantalisingly against his and sealed his fate. Then she stood up.

"Come on," she said. "It's getting late."

Two days later, he signed up for the Pals. One conversation with a pretty girl had led him to this hell, where he was waiting to die with only a rat for company.

Four

It wasn't the fact that Alfie found himself talking to the rat that surprised him. He would have talked to himself if there was no other alternative and it stopped him from going into a sleep from which he was convinced he would never wake up. The real surprise was that the rat talked back. At first, Alfie had been repulsed by the idea that the animal was perched on his boot, lapping at his blood, and had tried to shake his foot to dislodge it. The rat had clung for a while, but eventually hopped off and landed on the mud, where it sat, washing the blood of its muzzle with its paws. When it had finished, it regarded Alfie with shiny jet eyes.

"You don't look so good," it said. Its voice didn't sound the way Alfie would have expected a talking rat to sound. It had a Lancashire accent and sounded a lot like Jimmy Clayton.

"You spoke," he said, surprising himself by having a voice at all.

"I know," the rat replied. "And?"

"Rats don't speak."

"No, rats don't usually have anything much to say. There's a difference."

"Why are you speaking now?"

"Might as well. Another hour or two hanging there and you probably won't be telling anyone. You'll be as dead as Jimmy. You'll be dead as the rest of them."

"Someone might find me."

"Yeah," the rat said and there was a definite laugh in its voice. "Any minute now. I know you can't really look around much but let me tell you – there's nobody here. What's left of your lot have moved on and nobody else is going to come to this shit-hole. You're on your own, mate. Looks like you've had it."

"Then why are you still talking to me?"

"Because I like my meat fresh. Don't get any fresher than you. As soon as you're dead, you're lunch."

"What's stopping you now?"

"You're still alive, aren't you? I'm not going to start eating you while you're still alive. What do you think I am? Some kind of animal?"

"You are, aren't you?"

"Well, yes, but I don't always like being reminded of it. At the end of the day, we're all animals. Look at what your lot are doing. It's not exactly civilised, is it? Taking each other to bits for...what *are* you doing it for exactly?"

"We're doing it for the King. And for our country."

"And I'm sure your King would do the same for you, given half a chance. You are killing each other for a bit of land that you've managed to fill with mud and bodies. You're blowing each other apart over land that no one is going to want. You won't be able to grow any decent grain or anything here for years. That's what you're killing and dying for. Nothing. You're going to die out here and never get a chance to touch Daisy's tits and it's all for nothing. And you call *us* animals."

"How do you know about Daisy?"

"I've eaten your blood. I know all about you."

The rat pricked up its ears.

"Listen," it said, "the way I see it, is that you're thinking about dying too much. You think about dying and you'll die. Try thinking about living instead."

"You just said I was going to die."

"Got your attention, didn't it?"

"If I wasn't stuck here, I'd..."

"That's more like it. Still got a bit of fight in you. I only said you'd *probably* die. It's obviously not looking good, but I'm only a rat. What do I know? You could try shouting. There might be someone there. It's your choice. If you want to see Christmas, you need to do something about it now."

"I can't."

"Then you've definitely had it. Do you want to live?"

"Well – yes," Alfie's voice came out as a croak.

"I can't hear you, Private," the rat said and suddenly its voice sounded a lot like Sergeant Keenan, who had spent the first weeks out here yelling obscenities at the raw young recruits, but whose voice was silenced forever by a mortar on their first charge. "Do you want to live?"

"Yes Sarge."

"Louder!"

"*Yes Sarge!*"

"Good," the rat said in Jimmy's voice. "Don't worry about me, lad. There's enough other meat out here to keep me going for the rest of my life. Oh, and just so you know, nothing's free. There might be a price to pay for this one day."

"Like what?"

"You'll know it when you see it. Now get shouting."

With that, the rat was just a rat again, vermin sniffing around his bloody boots and waiting for him to die.

Shit, Alfie thought. *I've been talking to a rat. I'm losing my fucking mind.* All the same, he gathered what was left of his waning strength and started to shout.

Five

There was something pulling at his uniform, ripping the fabric and jerking his arms, making the barbs on the wire grip tighter. The only thought in his head was that the rat was back and this time it was feeding. Instinctively, he tried to raise his hand to bat it away, but he couldn't move and only twitched his fingers instead.

"Get me some wire cutters!" a voice shouted in his ear. "Quick! This one's alive!"

Then he blacked out again.

Six

He came to slowly at first. It wasn't a sudden jolt into consciousness, more like a dawning vague awareness that he was no longer asleep. He was disorientated, like he was emerging from a heavy dream and then he remembered and immediately wanted to go back to sleep again, needing oblivion to claim him again so he wouldn't have to think about what had happened to him. Sleep would not come, though, no matter how hard he tried.

He found it surprisingly difficult to open his eyes, as though his eyelids were heavy, but he when he finally did open his eyes, it made little difference. It was dark. He was lying on his back, looking up, but couldn't tell what he was looking at because his vision was blurred. All around he could hear groans and cries of pain. Somewhere nearby, someone was sobbing and someone else was repeating "No no no," over again in a hoarse voice that sounded like it would give out completely soon. Worse than the noise was the smell. His nose was assailed by a combination of putrid mud and smoke and something else, something rotten like decaying meat. He didn't know where that smell was coming from and hoped it wasn't from him. He tried to move, but nothing seemed to work the way it was supposed to and he hurt everywhere. There was pain in his arms, his chest and his face. He expected his left leg to hurt more than anywhere, but for some reason it didn't; it just felt numb.

A shadow fell across him and he could make out the shape of a person leaning over him. Something was pushed into his mouth and his teeth hit the rim of a cup. It was only when a trickle of water moistened his lips that he realised how dry his mouth was. He tried to take a sip, but the cup was pulled away.

"Easy," a female voice said. "You'll choke."

Alfie tried to say something in reply, but the words wouldn't come. His throat was too parched.

"Don't try to speak," the woman said. "I'll go and find a doctor." Then she was gone and he was on his own again.

He wasn't sure how long he was alone. It could have been half an hour, or it could have been hours. He might have dozed, but he wasn't sure. All around him the sounds of the suffering went on and on and he was glad that he couldn't speak because he wasn't sure that if he could make a noise, he too would make the sound of the dying. He could only hope that if he were dying, death would come quickly. Anything was better than this.

Seven

Sometime later, the woman came back. He thought it was the same woman, but his eyesight was still fuzzy and it was hard to hear her voice properly because he had a noise like rushing wind in his ears. He felt like he was underwater and wondered if this was how it was for the lads he saw drowning in the mud. There was a man with the woman, who pushed and poked at him, which made his wounds scream. The man was too hurried to be gentle. Through the whooshing in his ears, Alfie could catch some of what the man was saying, but the words barely made sense.

"Sorry, old chap..." he heard, and "...badly infected..." and "...had to take it off...save your life..." and finally "Sorry" again. The woman – he presumed it was the woman – laid a cool palm on his cheek, and then he was alone again.

It was a good hour or more before he summoned the courage to reach out a trembling hand to his left leg. He touched his thigh and it was there, solid and real and covered in whatever clothing his was wearing – it felt like the rough material of his uniform. He followed his thigh down towards his knee and felt...nothing. Where his knee should have been there was nothing, just a stump wrapped in what felt like bandages. He tried to touch it, but a bolt of pain shot up his thigh and he had to stop. He lay back, defeated. These people, doctors who were meant to heal, had killed him as surely as if that German bullet had gone through his head. He was done, finished. He couldn't go back home now. Daisy wanted him to come back a hero, not a cripple. He couldn't even work on the farm. Whoever heard of a one-legged farmer? He closed his eyes and in his head he cursed the war and the Germans and Daisy Atwell and Jimmy for making him go. Most of all, he cursed a fucking rat for making him want to live for *this*. He wished he had ground it into the mud while he still had a foot to do it with.

Eight

When he was asleep, which was a lot of the time, he kept seeing that rat. His dreams were indistinct and haunting, but in every one, that louse-ridden bag of fur and bones was there watching him, not doing anything, not speaking, just watching him with its button-black eyes. Sometimes when he was half awake, he would hear a scuffling, scratching sound near his head and was convinced the rat was with him. There must be plenty of rats around whatever place this was, though, and it couldn't be the same rat. He'd left it out there in the mud with half his knee and with the corpses of too many good men.

The strange thing was that before he knew his leg was gone, he had felt nothing apart from numb. Now he knew they had taken it, he could feel it all the time. It ached and itched and he wanted to scratch it so badly, but there was nothing there to scratch. A couple of times he had the oddest feeling, as though there were mud on his leg and it was sliding off. It had been a familiar feeling out there on the field, but not one he should be feeling now. He wanted to ask someone about it, but apart from when they came to feed him, spooning slop into his mouth like a bloody baby, nobody came near. His vision was clearing now and he could see people rushing about, dressed in makeshift doctors' and nurses' clothes, like kids playing dress-up, but they looked exhausted and grief-stricken and he couldn't make himself heard above the cries and screams of the other men who filled this place. In any case, part of him wanted them to stay away. If they came anywhere near, they might cut another bit of him off and he wanted to be left alone to die. At times he could feel the stump of his leg burning and he knew only too well that meant infection, as if the smell coming from it wasn't clear enough. Maybe the infection would take hold completely and he'd die in his sleep. The next time a doctor got close enough to look at him, they'd find him dead and chuck him outside, or whatever they did with the dead here. He hoped it would be soon and hoped it would be easy.

Nine

But death left him alone too. Two days later, as dawn was seeping through the gaps in what he now knew was a tent, they came and shipped him out. A couple of stretcher-bearers came and picked him up and carried him out of the tent into the open air.

"Your lucky day, son," one of them said, in an accent that sounded Scottish to Alfie. "You're going back to Blighty. Your war's over, Private."

"No," Alfie tried to say. "Leave me."

"Can't do that, wee man," the stretcher-bearer said. "They need the space. There's bloody hundreds coming in and they're worse than you."

They carried him down a track to the banks of a canal and loaded him onto a boat, a barge with a rough red cross painted on the side. He was crammed in amongst what looked like dozens of other men. To one side of him was one man who lay facing away, his back to Alfie, his shoulders moving up and down as he quietly sobbed. Alfie turned the other way and saw another man in a Private's uniform, tufts of red hair sticking out from the stained bandages that swathed his head and covered his eyes.

"Is someone there?"

Alfie was in no mood for conversation, so didn't answer, but the red-headed Private reached out, found his arm and grabbed it.

"Who's there?" he asked again.

"There's bloody loads of us," Alfie replied. "Too many."

"Where are we? They didn't tell me. It feels like we're moving."

"We're on a boat. Going home, they said. You can let go of my arm now."

The other soldier relaxed his grip but didn't let go completely.

"I'm Davey," he said. "Davey Morgan."

Oh Christ, Alfie thought. *Don't tell me your name. I don't need any mates out here.*

"What's your name?" Davey persisted.

"Alfie Sweeney."

"Pleased to meet you, Alfie." Alfie didn't reply. "I'm blind," Davey said and Alfie could detect an accent, probably Welsh. "Fucking flashbang went off in my face. One of ours it was. How stupid is that? Killed my mate and blinded me. Why are you here?"

"Fancied a bit of a rest," Alfie said, before he could stop himself, then relented. "Lost my leg."

"I'm sorry," Davey said. "That's bad. At least you're alive, eh? I think most of the lads I came out here with are dead. Haven't seen them for a while. Mind you, I can't see anything now, can I?" He laughed, which surprised Alfie, although he couldn't join in. *At least you're alive.* That was a fucking joke for a start. Alfie stopped speaking, hoping that Davey would lose interest and leave him alone. It didn't work for long.

"Could you do us a favour?" Davey asked.

"What's that?"

"I've never been on a canal before and I must be missing a lot with, you know, *these*," he gestured towards the bandages on his face. "Could you tell me what you can see?"

In truth, it was so gloomy inside the barge that Alfie couldn't really see much more than Davey. The windows were all covered, presumably so that the Germans couldn't see any lights and make it a target, but he knew that even if there was light, all he'd be able to see was a load of soldiers who were going home with bits missing, or their minds gone, young men like him who would never be the same again. If they survived the journey, that was, and the state a lot of them were in, they'd be lucky to get through the day. Alfie was tempted to tell Davey exactly what it was like and serve him bloody right for asking, but he didn't. Much as he had been brought up not to lie, there didn't seem any harm in it now. Even though he had never been on a barge either, he had lived in the country all his life and could imagine what it would be like. He described hedges and fields, just like the ones back in England, where the ground wasn't churned up into mud and shrouded in smoke and gas and dead soldiers. He described sunlight catching the ripples on the water and turning them gold and damsel flies flitting across the surface of the water and ducks dipping under the surface to fish. He tried to picture everything he could think of until tears began to sting his eyes. He tried to blink them back, even though he knew that Davey could not see them and kept talking until the young Welshman's head drooped and his breathing slowed, betraying the fact that he had fallen asleep. Only then did he allow himself to weep for all that he had lost.

Ten

When he had wept his eyes dry, he tried to sleep. He could hear Davey stirring and didn't feel like talking at the moment. He feared what might come out if he did. All the men on this barge had their own anguish and nobody wanted to hear his. He tried to block out the cries and whimpers and whispered conversations that were all around him and instead concentrated on the rhythmic thrum of the barge's engine and splash of the water against the hull. He thought he could hear gunfire in the distance, but then he heard that, real or imagined, whenever he closed his eyes. At some point he must have fallen asleep, because he dreamed of Jimmy, but it was not the healthy, happy friend he remembered. This Jimmy was in a mud and blood caked uniform, sitting silently in a trench, propped up against a pile of filthy sandbags. His right arm and shoulder had been torn away, and so had half his face. With his one good hand he was trying to force a cigarette into the ruin of his mouth. Perched on his left shoulder, gazing out with what could best be described as disapproval, was a scruffy, flea-bitten rat. The rat crouched, tensed and bared long yellow teeth. Then it jumped straight at Alfie, but he woke, gasping for air before it landed. He didn't try sleeping again for a while after that. He lay, staring at the roof of the barge, willing the infection he could feel in the stump of his leg to take over the rest of his body and end this misery once and for all.

Half his wish was granted. The infection did take hold and he spent the rest of the journey burning with fever, half-insane with delirium and finally, mercifully unconscious. While he was out cold, the barge reached its destination and Alfie, and the rest of the men who had survived the trip, were loaded onto a ship and taken across the Channel to England. There was no heroes' welcome, as they might have imagined when they joined up, only a fleet of ambulances and commandeered vans, waiting to take them on to their journey's end.

Eleven

When his fever broke, and he came to, everything felt different. The first thing he could feel was that he was no longer wearing his uniform. The scratchy, mud-stiffened khaki had been replaced by something softer and looser. He could still feel his wounds, but instead of hurting, they felt tight. There was an ache in the stump where his leg used to be, but nothing like the pain and fire he had felt before. He could no longer smell the sickly odour of infection, or indeed the stench of sweat and grime that had been so ever-present that he wondered if he could possibly be clean again. But he was clean and warm and in a room bathed in sunlight and thought that perhaps he might have died after all.

He lifted his head off his pillow (a *pillow*! That was novel, too) and looked around. He was in a large room and the sunlight he had seen was pouring in through a huge bay window. Apart from his own, there were five other beds in the room, all occupied by men who looked around his age or slightly older. A couple were asleep, one was reading a book, one was sitting on the edge of his bed, looking out of the window and one was just staring straight ahead, tears coursing unchecked down his cheeks. A young woman in a nurse's uniform was tending to the man who was looking out of the window, talking to him in a soft, quiet voice. When she had finished with him, she looked round, noticed that Alfie was awake and came over. She consulted her clipboard and nodded. She was young, like the other patients somewhere near Alfie's age, dark haired and pretty, though her face was pale and dark smudges under her eyes betrayed how tired she was. Then she smiled and for a moment, the exhaustion vanished.

"Private Alfred Sweeney, if our records are correct, which they often aren't."

"That's me," Alfie tried to say, but attempting to speak made him realise how dry his mouth was.

"I'll get you some water," the nurse said and poured some from a jug on a table by Alfie's bed. She sat on the edge of the bed and held the glass to his lips. "Sip," she said. He did, and it was the finest thing he had ever tasted. Greedily, he drank some more.

"Take it slowly," the nurse said. "You've been out for quite a while. Good to see you back with us."

"How long?" Alfie asked.

"I'm not completely sure. As long as you've been here, that's for sure. Now you're awake, I'll ask Doctor Shaw to come and see you. He'll be able to tell you more."

"What is this place? Hospital?"

"Sort of. You've got the honour of staying in Calvey Manor. His Lordship has graciously given over part of his ancestral home so we can look after you boys."

"You don't approve."

"No, it's good of him. But it shouldn't be necessary. There shouldn't be so many..." She stopped, glancing round as if fearful of being overheard. "I'm sorry. I'm speaking out of turn. I'll go and see if Doctor Shaw is free."

She put the glass down on the bedside table and hurried from the room.

"She's a little cracker, that one, isn't she?" It was the man two beds down who spoke. He was the one who had been reading but had now put his book down.

"She's...nice," Alfie replied.

"She's one of the best. Some of the others...Christ. There's one you definitely wouldn't let anywhere near you if you had a choice, 'specially when it comes to washing you. She looks like she'd rather rip the fucking thing off than wash it. John Callaghan, by the way. Call me Johnny."

"Alfie Sweeney. I'd get up, but I haven't got enough legs these days."

"I know. They said. Good to have a bit of conversation, though. These other lads are a bit quiet. He's okay," Johnny pointed to one of the sleeping men, "old Joe. He's a Sergeant, but you wouldn't know it. Sleeps a lot, though. The others don't talk.

You wouldn't know there's anything wrong with them, but they're gone in the head. Christ knows what they've seen."

"What's up with you?" Alfie asked.

"Same as you, but I went a bit further," Johnny said and pulled back his bedclothes to reveal that he was missing both his legs. "At least you can hop. I'm in a wheelchair for life."

"I'm sorry."

"Don't be. I'm glad to be out of it and back over here, even if I left my legs behind. There's too many'll not be coming home at all. At least this way, the bastards won't be sending us back out there. They reckon with a bit of rest and that I could even be going home soon."

"Where's home?"

"Liverpool. Can't you tell? What about you?"

"Lancashire. Out Chorley way."

"Sounds like the war's done us a favour, then."

"How come?"

"There's no way they'd let a couple of Northern lads stay in a place like this otherwise, is there? They'd send us packing!"

"How can you laugh about it?"

"Got to, haven't you? It's the only way through this if you don't want to end up like these lads. I don't reckon they'll ever go home while they're like this. They'll end up haunting this place, with the other ghosts."

"Ghosts?"

"So the lovely Nurse Kearney said. She might have been winding me up, though. She's a good laugh like that. She said there's a child who runs along the corridors upstairs giggling, but there's no kids here, not anymore. And a maid who walks through the wall in kitchen downstairs. There's a soldier, too, Civil War or something, just appears in the grounds and watches." Johnny paused for a second, then laughed. "'Course I reckon she's just trying to keep me awake so she's got company when she's on nights. No such thing as ghosts, is there?"

Twelve

Nurse Kearney didn't return for several hours, during which Alfie chatted with Johnny for a bit, and when that exhausted him, rested and tried to sleep. If he slept, he didn't dream. He must have dozed because he was suddenly aware that someone was gently shaking his arm.

"Sorry to wake you," Nurse Kearney said. "But we've managed to find Doctor Shaw and we don't want to lose him again."

Alfie looked up to see that there was a man standing next to the young nurse. He was stooped and grey-haired and looked almost too old still to be working. Like Nurse Kearney, he looked like he hadn't slept in days, and tiredness had carved out deep lines around his mouth and eyes. All the same, he managed a flicker of a smile.

"Anyone would think I hid deliberately," he said. "Too many patients and not enough doctors. But you don't want to hear my problems, Private. We're very glad to see you awake. Has Nurse Kearney told you anything?" Alfie shook his head. "Well, you were running a high fever when you were brought here about a fortnight ago and we were worried we might lose you for a bit. Your leg was badly infected, but we managed to get that sorted out, although I'm afraid you've lost a little bit more of it. We had no alternative, I'm sorry. If we hadn't done that, you might have lost the whole leg and with the facilities we have here, it's easily possible you wouldn't have survived. But here you are, and welcome. The plan, such as it is, is to get you to rest a bit and to strengthen the good leg, because that's going to be doing all the work from now on. With crutches, you should be able to get about, though you'll be in a wheelchair with the lovely Nurse Kearney or one of her colleagues wheeling you about at first. There's a games room downstairs that some of the men like to use and a lounge. And of course, there's the grounds. With a bit of luck, and if you put the work in, there's no reason why you can't go home before too long. Your other wounds have healed nicely, which is lucky. Barbed wire can be a bugger sometimes, but your wounds were nasty but not too deep. I know it doesn't feel like it, but you've been very lucky, Private."

"So people keep telling me."

"I suggest you listen to them. You're going to feel low and no one can blame you. You've been through the most terrible time and it's left its marks on you, not just on your body, but up here," he tapped his forehead. "Some of these poor chaps may never get their minds back, but that's for cleverer men than me to work out. I'm just a village doctor who thought he'd retired years ago. This damn war."

"Thank you," Alfie said. "Thanks for what you've done."

"I do what I can," Doctor Shaw said. "We all do. Now I'm sure you won't mind if I leave you in the hands of Nurse Kearney, here. I'll get back to see you when I can."

The doctor straightened up, almost, with a wince. He gave Alfie a vague salute, then left. Nurse Kearney watched him go, a frown of concern furrowing her brow.

"He's exhausted," she said. "I don't know when he finds time to sleep. He's such a good man. I don't know how he does it."

"What about you?" Alfie asked.

"I keep going," she replied. "Sleep and eat when I can. There's so much to do. Speaking of food, though, you must be starving. Let's see if we can rustle you up something to eat."

"Thank you, Nurse Kearney. Thanks for everything."

"It's Helen," she said, but raised her finger to her lips. "Don't tell anyone, though. I'd never hear the last of it."

Thirteen

Alfie spent the next couple of days resting or chatting with Johnny. There was another man in the bed between, but he was mentally absent and didn't notice that they spoke to each other across his prone body. The Sergeant, who Jimmy had said was all right, had been moved out of their room the day before, but nobody would say why.

The days were starting to settle into a routine, with meals at predictably regular times, and of predictable quality, though he had to admit that the food was better than he might have expected. The weather was mostly cloudy or wet, so he had no particular desire to venture outside. Helen, or one of the other nurses whose names he didn't know and who he didn't like as much, checked on him several times a day, to change dressings or to wash him, which he found highly embarrassing, but didn't seem to bother them. For some reason, he found the washing easier when it was one of the other nurses; there was something about Helen that made him feel shy. He still had dark thoughts and bad dreams, but there was something about being here that was making him feel very slightly better. Maybe it was the fact that he was a long way away from the Front, or maybe it was because there were so many lads here who were damaged more severely than he was. Some would die here, and some were ruined for life, either physically or mentally. Alfie was alive and could think, even if he would never walk again. He was so wrapped up in himself that he rarely thought of home, until the day Helen brought him paper, envelopes and a pen.

"You should write home," she said. "They won't know where you are and might think you're dead."

"And tell them what?" Alfie asked. "That I've only got one leg? That I'll never be of any use again?"

"That you're alive," Helen said. "Don't you think that's all they need to know? They'll have been worried sick. At least write to your mum and dad. They'll be so happy to hear from you, they won't care if you've got no arms or legs. What about a sweetheart? Is there someone special back home?"

"There is...someone," Alfie said, and then paused. Daisy probably wouldn't want to know him now, not in this state. "She wanted a hero. She won't want...*this*."

To his surprise, Helen laughed.

"You've got a funny idea about what a hero is," she said. "You were prepared to go and fight for your country, for all of us. You risked everything to try and keep the folk back home safe. If that doesn't make you a hero, I don't know what does."

"What about...?" he gestured towards the place where his leg used to be.

"Better a live hero with one leg than a dead hero. Write to them, Alfie. Doesn't have to be long, but just let them stop worrying."

After she had gone, he stared at the paper for a long time, not even sure how to begin. He wrote to his mum and dad first, because he thought that would be easier. He let the words come, telling them he was alive but had been injured and was being looked after and would write again soon. He didn't tell them what his injury was, or where he was (he couldn't tell them that because, apart from being in a big house somewhere, he didn't actually know where it was). He was about to finish the letter, but then thought about his old mate and wondered what Jimmy's folks and his wife Mary had been told. Poor Mary had only been wed a couple of weeks before Jimmy left and now she was a widow. He asked his parents to let Jimmy's family know he had been with him when he died, that he had passed quickly, but not before he had told Alfie how much he loved Mary. Alife felt bad at first, about telling such a barefaced lie but he couldn't tell the truth, that he'd seen Jimmy Clayton hit by a burst of machine gun fire and trampled into the mud by the rest of the advancing platoon. Alfie had wanted to go back for him but couldn't. There was no going back out there, just moving forward, gaining yards of worthless land.

Alfie finished that letter and addressed the envelope, then thought long and hard about what to say to Daisy. In the end, although he kept this letter simple too, it was the hardest thing he had ever written.

Dear Daisy,

Just to let you know that I am alive and back in England. I have been badly injured but I am trying to get better.

I think of you often and the times we had, but I am not the same man that I was when I left. I can't be the hero or the husband you wanted, so you are free. I hope you can find someone who will make you very happy.

With love,

Alfie

He debated whether to put a kiss on the end but decided not to. Even the 'love' wasn't really true. When he thought about his mum and dad, he felt an ache to get back to them. When he thought of Daisy, he felt nothing at all, just the shadow of a memory. It wasn't only the lack of a leg that made him a different man now.

Fourteen

He saw the ghost for the first time that night. It might have been because he was resting so much during the day that he found it difficult to sleep at night. In the day-time, there were always doctors and nurses talking as they bustled down the corridor outside Alfie's room and he could often hear patients moving around too. Without being able to see them, he could tell which ones were walking or shuffling, and which ones were using crutches or wheelchairs. Hopefully, before very long, he would be one of them. At night, however, the house went quiet. The staff dropped their voices to a whisper, if they conversed at all, but the only other sounds were occasional shouts from patients in other rooms. Alfie had once asked Helen how many other patients there were in the Manor, but she hadn't answered, which he took to mean that either she wasn't prepared to say or didn't know. As he hadn't been outside yet, he had no idea how big the house was, but from what little he knew about manor houses, he thought it would probably be very big indeed, and if every room had six patients in it like this one, there must be dozens of men here, if not hundreds. How the nursing staff coped with them all, he could only imagine. It was no wonder they looked tired.

When the night-time hush fell over the Manor, it was harder for Alfie to distract himself from thoughts of his old life back home, or from the horrors he had witnessed on the Somme. He wasn't much of a reader, never had been, so books were no good to him, but even if they were, there wasn't enough light to read by. It was a strange thing; if he dozed during the day, he didn't dream, or if he did, he didn't remember. It was only when he slept at night that the dreams came. Some nights he dreamed that he was in his bed in the Manor, but there was something in the wall behind him, something scratching and scrabbling, and he knew with the certainty of dreams that it was a rat and it was trying to get out. He always woke before it did. In other dreams, he was back on the battlefield, suspended on the barbed wire, with shells and gunfire getting closer and closer. In those dreams, he felt every wound, from the barbs piercing his flesh to the agony of his shattered knee. Once, he could feel something moving, trying to force itself into the hole the bullet had opened in his knee and he knew that if he looked down he would see that the rat was gnawing its way into his leg. He kept his eyes fixed on the fire and the flashes ahead and didn't look down. He woke from these dreams sobbing and on one occasion, screaming. That night, his anguish had woken Johnny up and brought one of the night nurses running. The other patients remained catatonic, lost in their own worlds. Johnny muttered something, turned over and went back to sleep. The nurse stayed with Alfie, holding his hand and softly reassuring him until he calmed down. Nights like that made him fearful of going to sleep and he lay in the dark, waiting for dawn.

The first time he saw the ghost, it must have been a dream, although at the time it felt very real indeed. He was sitting in a chair by his room's large bay window, looking out onto the grounds. When he recalled it later, there could be no doubt that this was a dream, because as yet, he had not been out of his bed, let alone venture as far as the window. Helen had told him that there was a wheelchair waiting for him when he was ready, but as yet, he hadn't wanted to try, as if needing a wheelchair would be the final admission that he could no longer walk without assistance. In his dream, the Manor's grounds were partially illuminated by a pale silver moon and he could make out an expanse of grass, punctuated by smudges of shrubs. The grass was bordered by trees, whose branches made spiky shadow puppet shapes against the moon. As Alfie looked out, trying to accustom his eyes to the dark, he made could make out what looked like the figure of a person standing near the trees. It was a man but dressed like no man he had seen before. He appeared to be dressed in a tunic, breeches and boots and under one arm, he carried a domed object which was clearly made of metal by the way the moonlight caught it and made it glint. There was something hanging at the man's side and at first Alfie thought it was a swagger stick, like the officers carried in France, but it was longer than that and Alfie could swear it was a sword. The figure had its back to Alfie at first, but then slowly turned to face him. The face was indistinct, partly because of the distance, but partly because the whole figure looked insubstantial, like it was made out of smoke. Alfie thought he could make out a beard, but more than that, he couldn't be sure. The last Alfie remembered of the dream was that he was still looking out of the window and the figure was still standing rigidly to attention by the trees, looking back. Then the figure was gone and Alfie woke up. He didn't feel afraid of what he had seen, merely curious and inexplicably sad.

Fifteen

The next morning, when Helen came round with breakfast, he tentatively asked her if the wheelchair she had mentioned might perhaps still be available.

"Really?" she said, with a beam of genuine delight. "That's marvellous, Alfie. I'm so glad. I'll get the breakfast rounds done and go and fetch it as soon as I can. I'll tell Doctor Shaw, too. I have no doubt he'll agree."

True to her word, she returned an hour or so later, pushing a contraption that looked like it had not seen service since Victoria was on the throne.

"I know," Helen said, catching the dismay on his face. "It's the best I could find. Honestly, you should see some of the others. They're all donated, but they work. It's not going to collapse and throw you onto the floor, I promise. Will you still try?"

"I'll try," Alfie replied, though the prospect filled him with dread.

"Good. Now, before you do, I have to warn you. You will have lost a lot of strength in your good leg. You haven't used it for a long time, and it probably won't take your weight at first. I'll have to take all your weight."

"You?"

"Yes me." Helen gave him a stern look. "I know I'm not tall, Alfie. You don't have to say. But let me tell you, I'm a lot stronger than I look. I've hauled around much bigger lads than you."

"I'll bet you have," Alfie said and smiled despite himself. Helen, it turned out, was not just strong, but also as capable of barking order as any officer he had come across. He followed her instructions and sat up, then shuffled his backside along as close to the edge of the bed as he dared.

"Swing your leg round," she said, "but don't try and stand."

"Swing it?" Alfie said. "I can't feel it."

Helen gave him a not particularly light slap on the thigh.

"Feel that?"

"Yes!"

"Good. Now swing your leg round."

Alfie obeyed, and for the first time in weeks, felt solid ground beneath his foot. Helen pushed the wheelchair as close as to the bed as she could get it.

"Right," she said, and stood so close to him that he could feel her breath on his face and smell a faint, lingering trace of soap on her skin. "Put your arms around my neck and clasp your hands together. Pretend we're dancing."

"That's something else I'll never do again," Alfie said.

"Sorry. That was tactless."

"Don't be. I was a bloody awful dancer." He put his arms around her neck and held each of his wrists with the opposite hand. "Like this?"

Helen nodded and Alfie was suddenly acutely aware that he hadn't been this close to a woman since the last time he saw Daisy, and he didn't even know how long ago that was. He tried to think of Helen not as a woman, but as a nurse, a professional who did this all the time with countless men, but when he could feel her hair against his cheek, it made it difficult. Then she spoke again and he forced himself to concentrate.

"Slowly now," she said. "Lean on me."

Alfie tried to stand, but his leg felt like it was made of rubber and he fell back onto the bed.

"I can't!" he said. "Fucking leg doesn't work. Sorry."

"Don't talk like that. There's nothing wrong with that leg. It's just not used to working, that's all. Now come on, let's try again."

It took four attempts, with Alfie growing increasingly frustrated each time. Helen remained calm and reassuring, though and wouldn't let him give up. Finally, he gritted his teeth and forced himself upright, balancing precariously on one leg, and using Helen for a support. With her help, he managed to turn around and sat down in the wheelchair so heavily that, had Helen not steadied it in time, it might have tipped over backwards. By the time they had finished, they were both red-faced and breathing heavily.

"Look at the state of you," called Johnny, who had been watching with some amusement from his own bed. "You know what you look like you've been up to, don't you?"

"You mind your business, Johnny Callaghan," Helen shot back, but placed a hand on Alfie's shoulder and squeezed. It was supposed to send a message, he thought, but he really wasn't sure what the message was. Now he was in the wheelchair, he wasn't sure what he was supposed to do next. Helen provided the answer.

"Do you fancy a bit of fresh air?" she asked.

Sixteen

As Helen pushed him down the hall towards the Manor's front door, Alfie felt inexplicably anxious at the thought of going outside. He knew there was no reason for it, but he felt as though, once he was out of the safety of his room, all eyes would be on him, that everyone would want to have a look at the one-legged freak who was supposed to come back from the Front as a hero, but now needed a nurse to push him around. They hadn't got very far down the hall before he realised that his fears were unfounded. They passed other men who were also relying on a wheelchair and a nurse to get about and most were more severely injured than he was. One was missing an arm as well as a leg, one was like Johnny, with both legs gone and a couple were staring vacantly out of the shells their bodies had become, their heads lolling from side to side as they were pushed along.

"It's evil," Helen said, apparently reading his mind. "This war. All these men should be in the prime of their lives, getting themselves sweethearts and settling down. Now look at them. This bloody war will ruin a generation and it's not done yet."

"We thought we were doing what's right," Alfie said. "They never said what it would be like."

"You were sold a lie. May God forgive them for doing this to you all because I can't."

"There wasn't much sign of God out there. It was more like hell."

Helen stopped the wheelchair, came round so that she was in front of Alfie and crouched down beside him. She gently took his hand.

"You're safe now," she said. "You know that, don't you?"

"I think I do. Mostly. Part of me thinks I should still be out there. If other lads are still there, fighting and dying, I should be there with them."

"What are you going to do? Run the Germans over in your chair? You've done your bit and look what it's cost you. You're better off going home to your family and that girl you wrote to."

"She didn't write back. I didn't think she would. What have I got to offer her?"

"Plenty. It's only a leg, Alfie. Your face is okay and you're not a bad looking lad. This is the start, now. Another couple of days and we'll have you up on crutches, then there'll be no stopping you."

"You think so?"

"I do. You've got to, Alfie. You're not like some of these other poor boys. We've got to get you moving and get you home. You've got too much going for you to end up as one of the ghosts haunting this place."

Helen stood up and was about to go round to the back of the chair again, but Alfie caught her hand and stopped her.

"What do you mean? Ghosts?"

"Nothing. It's just...just an expression."

Helen tried to pull away, but he kept hold of her hand and wouldn't let her go.

"No it wasn't. Have you seen something?" She turned her face away, but Alfie persisted. "What have you seen?"

"Not here. Come on, let's go outside."

He let her go and they continued down the hall to the door. The large, wooden main door of the Manor was open and Helen steered Alfie through it, but he was dismayed to see that they were at the top of a wide flight of stone steps, which led down onto a gravel driveway.

"We can't get down there!" Alfie protested, but Helen pointed out several other wheelchair-bound patients, who were already being escorted round the grounds by nurses.

"They managed it," she said. "Hold tight and lean back. This is going to be bumpy."

She tilted the wheelchair back and Alfie was briefly worried that it would fall over completely, but once more, Helen took his weight and as carefully as she could, manoeuvred him down, one step at a time. All the same, he was considerably relieved when the wheels touched the gravel. It was then that he noticed how much colder it was outside. There was definite autumnal nip in the air; between the trenches and being unconscious, he'd missed summer this year. He shivered.

"Are you all right?" Helen asked. "Do you need a blanket or anything?"

"I just need to get used to it. I've not been outside for a bit. So go on then," he said. "Tell me about the ghosts."

"It's just stories," she said. "Come on, every old house like this is going to have ghost stories, isn't it? Doesn't mean they're really haunted."

"Doesn't mean they're not, either."

"Do you really believe in ghosts? A sensible lad like you?"

"I didn't. But I saw some things out there..." He stopped himself from saying *like a talking bloody rat*. She wasn't ready for that. "I saw some things, is all. Things that make you wonder. There's stuff I dreamed and stuff I know I didn't."

"I can't imagine what you saw. Any of you."

"You don't...you don't think about it at the time. It's just how it is. It's only now...I see it all the time. When I close my eyes."

Helen rested her hand on his shoulder.

"You're safe now."

She wheeled him across the drive and up onto the grass. The air smelled fresh and clear and somewhere a thrush was singing. There hadn't been any birds singing in France, just the constant whine of shells, the rattle of gunfire and sometimes the silence. The silence was worse because you knew something was coming, you just didn't know when.

Alfie realised that they were now standing on the grass he had seen in his dream, looking towards the trees. They looked different to how they had looked in the moonlight, smaller somehow and he wondered how he knew what they looked like at all.

"So what have you seen, Helen? Here, I mean."

"It's going to sound so silly. You'll laugh."

"I won't."

"You will. It was the other night. Tuesday? No, it was Monday."

"Go on," Alfie said, though he didn't really know when Tuesday was, or Monday, or what day it was now.

"I was on my break and I came out for a smoke. It was, I don't know, round midnight. Late, anyway. I saw someone standing over there by the trees. I thought it might have been one of the lads, but they're not allowed out at night, only the staff and we don't go any further than the drive. I called out, in case, you know, it was one of the *confused* lads, because they can wander sometimes. But he – I'm sure it was a man – wasn't one of ours. He wasn't dressed right. Sorry, I'm not explaining it very well."

"He didn't look like he was from now. He looked older."

"Yes! That's exactly it. How did you know?"

"Because I've seen him too. In a dream, it was, but I saw him. Looked like he was watching me."

"That's what I sort. It made me feel a bit funny, so I came back in. Couldn't stop thinking about him though. I started to think I'd imagined it, but I heard Elsie, one of the other nurses talking about it. Sounds like a few people have seen him."

"I wonder who he is," Alfie said, half to himself.

"Doesn't seem much point asking him. Don't think he's the talkative type. Some of the other girls think it's funny, but I think it's sad."

"He's just another lost soldier," Alfie said. "Like the rest of us."

"You're not lost," Helen said. "There's plenty who are, but you were found. Now come on, let's go back in. Don't want you catching your death."

As she pushed him back to the steps and hauled him up them one at a time, Alfie thought about that expression *catch your death*. Death wasn't something you caught; it was something that caught you, caught everyone in the end. It hadn't caught him yet.

Seventeen

Over the next week, trips around the grounds became part of Alfie's daily routine. Sometimes it was Helen who took him, sometimes it was another nurse called Maggie, who liked to talk about her boyfriend all the time and how he didn't like how much time she spent working at the Manor, looking after a lot of other men. He didn't get that most of the men weren't capable of doing anything anymore. Alfie had the impression that Maggie wasn't going to have a boyfriend for much longer, but he pretended to listen and said nothing, even when she paused for breath and gave him a chance to speak.

He didn't talk to Helen about the ghost again, either. He wanted to think about that for a bit first. Instead, they talked about other things, like the farm and his family. Helen was from Birmingham, and Alfie got the impression that Calvey Manor wasn't too far away from there, the way she talked. She'd never been as far North as Lancashire and asked him about the countryside as if it was a foreign country. She never asked him about the one foreign country he had been to, for which he was grateful. Talking brought back memories and he wanted to forget as much as he could. She told him about her own life; she was an only child, which she said she'd hated when she was growing up because all her friends had brothers and sisters and she only had her parents at home. Her dad was a teacher and her mum looked after the home and they were both too busy to play with her. When her friends were off doing things with their families, she was left on her own, reading or making up her own games. Now she was glad she had no brother to worry about or to mourn.

Alfie wasn't sure if he was seeing something that wasn't there, but he had the impression that Helen talked to him in a different way to how she talked to the other men in her care. With the others she was all efficiency but it felt like she opened up to Alfie more. He couldn't be sure, though. Daisy was the only girl he'd known and you couldn't really compare anyone to her. He liked Helen and got on well with her. He'd even once asked her, as casually as he could, if she had a sweetheart back in Birmingham. She laughed and said no, and even joked that she hoped there'd be some left to pick from once this was all over. Alfie didn't press it any further. Nice as she was, it wasn't like he had anything to offer her. Time was, he'd had a job and one day might inherit a farm, but now he had nothing. For as long as he was at the Manor, it was good to have someone to talk to and that would have to be enough.

Eighteen

That night, Alfie saw the ghost again. He spent most of his time in his wheelchair, which meant he could now push himself over to Johnny's bed, where they whiled away the time playing cards with a pack Helen had conjured up from somewhere. For all his bluster, Johnny tired easily and once he had settled down to sleep, Alfie pushed himself over to the window to watch as dusk fell over the grounds.

From his vantage point, he watched as Helen and a couple of other nurses emerged from the Manor and stood on the gravel drive, passing a cigarette around. The two other nurses were chatting away to each other, gesturing animatedly with their hands, but Helen stood slightly apart from them, only interacting with them when it was her turn for the cigarette. Alfie watched them finish up and disappear back inside and out of sight. When he looked back up towards the grounds, the pale, insubstantial figure of the soldier was standing by the trees. Alfie squinted, trying to make out more detail, but the figure was facing away from him and seemed to fade in and out. Then the figure slowly turned towards him and just for a second, his eyes met Alfie's and Alfie felt a wave of deep sadness wash over him, before the soldier disappeared as suddenly as he had appeared. Alfie watched and waited for what seemed like a long time, but the soldier didn't come back. Alfie went back to his bed and managed, with some difficulty, to get himself into it. He lay there not wanting to sleep, for fear that the soldier's ghostly face would haunt his dreams, but he slept and dreamed of nothing.

He was woken after what seemed like no time at all by a commotion nearby. A screen had been pulled around the bed between his and Johnny's and there was obviously something going on behind. He could hear voices whispering urgently to one another, but after a while, the whispers stopped and Doctor Shaw and a nurse Alfie didn't recognise, emerged solemnly from behind the screen. The nurse was silently weeping and Doctor Shaw led her out of the room. From the other side of the screens, Alfie heard Johnny's voice.

"That's another one gone, then," he said. "I don't reckon any of us are getting out of here alive."

Nineteen

They took the body away shortly afterward. Either Doctor Shaw or the nurse had covered its face with a sheet and two men Alfie didn't recognise loaded it onto a wheeled stretcher without any word or ceremony. He watched them go and pondered on Johnny's words. *No,* he thought, *I* am *getting out of here alive.* He was not going suffer the indignity of being carted away like that, to be buried God knows where. He was going to get out of here, walking any way he could, but there was something he needed to do before he could. For that, he needed Helen's help.

It was Maggie who brought the breakfast in the morning. Alfie felt bad tempered, through lack of sleep and because she wasn't Helen and was more off-hand with her than he intended. He regretted it after she was gone and vowed to apologise next time he saw her. The nurses worked in terrible conditions and didn't deserve patients who acted like spoiled brats when they didn't get what they wanted. It wasn't until the afternoon that Helen came round. She looked flustered and unhappy but did her best to smile.

"What's wrong?" Alfie asked.

"Nothing," Helen replied, trying not to meet his eyes. "I'm fine." Her own eyes were red-rimmed and she had clearly been crying.

"Tell me," Alfie said.

"I shouldn't say. We're not supposed to. We're supposed to smile and get on with it."

"What's happened, Helen? You can talk to me, you know. Who am I going to tell?"

Helen glanced over at Johnny, but he seemed to be snoozing. His eyes were shut, at any rate. All the same, she lowered her voice to a near-whisper.

"It's just this place," she said. "Sometimes I don't know how much longer I can stand it. We lost another four last night. Four! We're doing all we can for them. All the staff are dead on their feet but the poor lads keep coming. They say there's another couple of dozen coming today and where are we going to put them? We can't look after the ones we've got!"

"I've no complaints."

"I know. None of you complain, not the ones who can speak, anyway. We just need to get you on your feet and you'll be on your way."

"I want to start," Alfie said. "I want to start using crutches. Today."

Helen looked surprised for a second and then gave Alfie the first real smile she had given him since she had arrived. He thought it made her beautiful and couldn't help but smile back.

"Really? Alfie, that's marvellous! Why? Is there a reason?"

"You need the bed," Alfie said, then became serious. "I saw him last night."

"Who?" Helen looked at the empty bed next to Alfie's.

"No, not him, though I saw that too. *Him.* Our friend outside. The soldier."

"Did you? Are you sure? You weren't dreaming again?"

"No, I saw him. He was standing there by the trees, just as you said. He reminded me of something. It took me a while, but I know what it was now."

"What?"

"He looked like the lads who stood watch. They'd stand there for hours, hardly moving in case they missed something. I did it a few times myself. You daren't move. You hardly dare blink. You just stand there like a bloody statue, watching. That's what he reminded me of."

"Do you think that's what he's doing?"

"I don't know. It feels right, though. He looks lost and sad, like he was left there on watch but no one came. I need to talk to him, but I can't do it in a wheelchair like a cripple. I have to be standing up. Will you help me?"

"As much as I can. Of course I will."

Twenty

The first time he tried, he fell.

He thought it would be easy. He thought he could lean on the crutch and use it to replace his missing leg, and, although with Helen's help, he was able to stand upright, as soon as he tried to move, the crutch went one was and his good leg went the other. He tried to reach out for the bed as he fell, but missed and went crashing to the floor. He cursed, then remembered his manners and apologised to Helen, who tried not to laugh. She helped him to get back up and sit on the bed and once he had got his breath back, he tried again.

The second time he tried, he fell.

Once more, he was able to stand, but when he tried to move, his leg buckled and the crutch skidded away from him before he could steady himself. This time he fell sideways onto the bed. Helen took his arm and between them they got him sitting up. He immediately took hold of the crutch and had another try.

The third time he tried, he fell. And the fourth.

He was about to try for a fifth time, when Helen stopped him. By now he was bathed in sweat and his jaw hurt from clenching his teeth.

"That's enough, Alfie," she said. "You've tried. It will get easy and you *will* do it, but maybe not today. Rest now and we'll try again tomorrow."

"But the soldier..." Alfie protested.

"He's not going anywhere. He's dead, Alfie. But you're not and I'm not having you kill yourself trying to walk before you're ready. We'll try again tomorrow, I promise."

Reluctantly, he agreed. He tried to persuade Helen to leave the crutch when she went, but she refused. He said it would help him get in the wheelchair, but it was obvious that she didn't believe him. Even though she had frustrated his plans, he had to smile when she said, "Do you really think I don't know you by now? Get some rest."

Rest didn't come easily. His body ached from the effort and the armpit which had taken the strain of the crutch felt bruised. He was angry with himself for failing and struggled not to be angry with Helen for stopping him from going on. He lay on his bed, staring at the cracks in the ceiling and forced his breathing to slow down. As it did so, he began to feel calmer. Helen was right, of course. It was foolish to try to do too much at once. His body had been through a great deal although he was stronger than he had been, he was still nothing like the man who had spent afternoons chopping wood on the farm, or who could haul a reluctant cow in for milking. He doubted he would ever been anywhere near that man again, but he was damned if he wasn't going to do all he could to be better than this. But maybe not today.

Later that evening, as dusk lengthened the shadows of the trees in the grounds, the soldier appeared again. Alfie watched from the window as he kept his lonely vigil by the trees, saw again the sadness in his eyes when he turned around to face the Manor.

Soon, Alfie thought. *I'll be there soon.*

Twenty-One

The next day, he managed two steps. It took him several tries, but he was determined that it wasn't going to beat him. Even though Helen was still bearing most of his weight, he managed to balance first on his leg, then on the crutch. His bruised armpit screamed at him when he leaned on the crutch, but he stayed upright. Then he did it again. It was only when he stopped and realised how far he had moved away from his bed and so how far he had to go back that his courage deserted him. When Helen asked him if he'd had enough, he admitted that he had. She had to let go of him to fetch the wheelchair and in those horrible few seconds that he was left standing on his own, he was terrified that he was going to lose his balance and fall again. But Helen didn't let him fall. Her reassuring hand was once more on his arm, steering him back into the wheelchair, where he gratefully sat down. He wanted to try again straight away, but Helen shook her head firmly.

"No," she said. "Not today. That was a massive step, but don't rush it. We'll do a bit more each day."

"It'll take me a month to get to the door at this rate," Alfie replied, sullenly.

"If it does, it does. I know you want to be up and about as soon as you can, but we've got to do it safely. What if you fall and hurt your good leg? It could set you back weeks and we don't want that, do we?"

"No, I suppose we don't."

"Right then. You be a good little soldier and do as you're told."

Alfie was wrong. It took him four days to get as far as the door of the room and back. Each night when he sat and looked out of the window, the spectral form of the soldier was there, keeping his lonely watch and giving Alfie the incentive to get moving. Every night, Alfie repeated his silent promise that he would be there soon, and every night the soldier turned, gazed back at him and then vanished. Every day, Alfie made more progress and just over a week after he started, he made it down the corridor and reached the front door of the Manor. He was never on his own, however, because Helen stayed with him all the time, her hand on or near his back, just in case he wobbled or became anxious. Her very presence took his anxiety away. He trusted her as more than just a nurse; she was his friend. On the day he reached the front door, she hugged him in delight and kissed him on the cheek and it was all he could do to stay upright.

"I'm so proud of you," she said, her breath warm against his ear.

"I couldn't do it without you," he said. "Thank you."

"Well, you're going to have to, sooner or later. I'm not always going to be there. You won't need me at all soon. You'll be able to do it by yourself."

The thought of that saddened him. Deep down he knew it was coming, that one day he would leave here and Helen would have other patients who needed her more, but he had come reply on her support and encouragement. More than that, he had grown very fond of her, possibly even loved her, though he could never say it. Half the men here must have been a bit in love with her and there could be no future in it. When he left the Manor and went home, he would never see her again, so it was best not to get too attached.

She broke the hug first and made a show of adjusting her uniform.

"The state of me," she said. "Let's get you back to your room. You go first. I'll be right behind you, but let's see how you go on your own."

The thought of that almost made him panic, but he took a breath, imagined that Helen was by his side, and slowly made his way back to his room. Once he was back in his wheelchair, Helen looked at her watch.

"Would you look at the time? I've got to go. There are other patients here than you, Alfie Sweeney."

"Will you leave the crutch?"

"Not this time. I know why you want it and you're not quite there yet. You're not ready to get down those steps yet, and if you fall down them, that'll be it."

She must have seen the look of disappointment on his face and relented.

"I'll tell you what," she said. "I'm not working tomorrow night unless anything happens. If you can get to the front door and back on your own tomorrow, I'll come back at night and help you with the steps. Then you can do what you have to do. Mind, if anyone sees us, we'll have to come back in. I'm not losing my job over a bloody ghost."

"That's fair. Thank you."

That night, Alfie's plan to see the soldier was frustrated by Johnny, who for once wouldn't go to sleep. He was much too keen to tease Alfie about Helen.

"You got your own personal nurse, these days, Alf?" he asked.

"She's helping me walk," Alfie replied. "She looks after other lads too."

"Bet she doesn't spend as much time with them. I reckon she's sweet on you, mate."

"She's just helping me. She'll be done soon."

"I wouldn't mind a pretty girl like that looking after me. I just get that Maggie."

"Maggie's all right."

"She's bloody not. She's got cold hands for a start. Bet that Helen's hands are warm, eh?"

"Leave it, Johnny. She's a nurse. She's got a job to do."

"Tell you what, if I had her looking after me, I wouldn't be in any hurry to get better."

"I said leave it," Alfie snapped. He felt just about ready to punch Johnny's stupid smirking face. "I want to get out of here. She's helping me do it. Now fucking shut up about it."

"Calm down, Alf," Johnny said, raising his hands. "I'm only pulling your leg. At least you've still got one to pull." He paused. "You *do* like her, don't you?"

"It's past your bedtime, Johnny," Alfie said and wheeled himself back to his own bed. As he did so, he sent cast a glance towards the window. *I'm sorry,* he thought. *Tomorrow.*

Twenty-Two

The next morning, Alfie waited as patiently as he could for Helen to come. Since he had been trying to walk with the crutch, he had been so exhausted by the end of the day that, once he had completed his vigil for the soldier and gone to his bed, he slept right through. He woke an hour or so before breakfast was brought round, but he slept deeply and usually the bad dreams stayed away. Last night, however, they were back. He dreamed about the Somme, about the look on Jimmy's face as the machine guns tore him apart and he dreamed that he was stuck on the barbed wire again, only this time, the wire was growing out of his flesh like a malignant bramble. He woke from this latter dream sweating and crying out and for a few horrible moments his whole body was paralysed, as if the wire had turned his veins to steel and rooted him to the bed. When he could finally move again, he lay awake in fear of returning to that horror if he should go back to sleep. He must have dozed off again, because he dreamed he was lying in his bed, but once more, there was the noise of something in the walls behind his head, scrabbling to get out. He could hear the plaster crumbling and when he dared to look round, he could see cracks in the wall and, where the plaster had fallen away, small black claws were stealing their way through. When he woke this time, he was disorientated, no longer completely certain whether he was awake or dreaming and had to reach out a tentative, trembling hand to touch the wall to make sure. Once he knew he was safe, and that the only sounds he could hear were Johnny's snoring and the birds outside starting their dawn chorus, he lay back on his pillow and forced his eyes to stay open for what remained of the night.

Neither Helen nor Maggie was on breakfast duty that morning. It was nurse he hadn't seen before, who looked like she should still be in school. She had clearly only just started and kept apologising for everything she did, even though as far as Alfie could see, she wasn't getting anything wrong. Her constant apologies irritated him, but he tried not to show it, in case it made her apologise even more. Although he had little appetite, he forced his breakfast down; he was going to need all his strength if he were to prove to Helen that he could walk without help. Once he had finished, and the young nurse had collected his tray, he lay waiting for the tortuous time to tick by until Helen came. He spent the time concentrating furiously on the muscles of his leg and his arms, as if he could force energy into them by willpower alone. By the time she finally arrived, he felt so tense that he had to bite his tongue so as not to snap at her for being late and say something he would surely regret.

But she gave him that smile, full of kindness and concern and any resentment over the length of his wait disappeared completely.

"Are you ready for this?" she asked.

"Yes," he replied. "I am." He swivelled round to sit on the edge of the bed and reached out for the crutch. "Do you want to see?"

"For goodness' sake, Alfie, take your time. You're not going to do anyone any good if you're flat on your face. I've had enough of picking you up off the floor. Just go steady. It's not a race." Alfie gave her a quick smile, but instead of replying, took off down the corridor as quicky and steadily as he could. When he reached the door, he did a swift about face without stopping and came back. He came to a halt in front of Helen, leaned hard on the crutch and saluted. She beamed and saluted back.

"Good work, Private Sweeney," she said.

"Tonight then," he replied.

"Yes. All right. Tonight it is."

Twenty-Three

Alfie was restless for the rest of the day. He played some cards with Johnny, who seemed to have forgotten about their disagreement, though Helen wasn't mentioned again. Whether Johnny thought better of it, or whether the joke was now wearing a bit thin, Alfie didn't know, but didn't intend to find out. It was hard enough to concentrate on the game and Johnny seemed happy enough to be comfortably winning every hand. Alfie wasn't bothered either way. They were only playing for matchsticks and he didn't care how many he lost. He had more important things on his mind and simply wanted the day to be over so that he could go and do what he needed to do. Inevitably, this made the day drag more than just about any other day since he arrived here.

He ate his meals without complaint and tried to doze when he could, and when his mind would let him, but whenever he closed his eyes, all he could think about was the task ahead. When the time came for the lights to be turned out in his room, he was wide awake and watchful. Johnny had settled down early, and the other patients in the room were not really aware of their surroundings, so nobody noticed that Alfie didn't get undressed and into bed. He sat in his wheelchair and waited for Helen.

Sometime near midnight, the door to the room creaked open, and he could see Helen silhouetted against the wedge of light from the corridor outside. She closed the door quietly and crept over to his bed.

"You know I could get sacked for this?" she whispered.

"I'll take all the blame," Alfie replied. "If anyone sees us, we can just say I wouldn't settle without a bit of fresh air or something. We'll say I didn't give you much choice."

"If anyone sees us, we'll be coming straight back and that'll be that. You're not my only patient, you know. I'm not losing my job for you."

"I wouldn't ask you to. Don't worry. It'll be fine."

"Come on then, let's get this done."

Alfie used his crutches to pull himself upright and then followed Helen to the door. She gestured to him to wait, while she eased the door open, grimacing at the creak, and peered outside. She shook her head and went out into the corridor. Alfie waited, listening to hushed voices outside the room and trying not to hold his breath. A few minutes later, she returned.

"All clear," she whispered. "I had to send Betsy off on a wild goose chase, but it should give us enough time. Let's go, Private."

Alfie gave her a mock salute, gripping his crutch with his armpit. He almost lost his balance but grabbed his crutch again and steadied himself. Helen flashed him a disapproving look, but he grinned and followed her out into the corridor.

The corridor, which bustled with activity during the day, seemed to be deserted as Helen led him to the front door. When they reached it, she produced a bunch of keys from somewhere in her apron and quietly unlocked the door.

"I'm not supposed to have these," she said, "and they've got to be back in half an hour or I could really get into trouble."

"I understand," Alfie replied.

"As long as you do. Now go and do what you have to. I'll wait here. Be careful on those steps."

"I will. I promise."

Helen glanced over her shoulder again, then opened the front door and let him out. He hadn't expected it to be quite so cold outside, but then it had been a long time since he had been outside at night. The sky was clear and speckled with stars and a half-moon was just visible through the trees and gave him just enough light to see where he was going. He took the steps down to the drive carefully, one at a time, resisting the urge to hurry, mindful of Helen's warning. If he fell, he would certainly have difficulty getting up and wouldn't be able to call to Helen for help, for fear of getting her into trouble. There were only a few steps, but until he was safely on the drive, it felt like descending a mountain. He sighed with relief when he felt the gravel under his foot and set off across the drive to towards the grass and the trees. As yet there was no sign of the ghost soldier.

Alfie made his way across the grass nearly as tentatively as he had navigated the steps, only too aware that if he caught his crutch in a hole or a dip, he could be thrown onto the ground with no chance of stopping himself. He reached the area under the trees where he had observed the soldier from the window, stopped and looked around. He was still on his own. He didn't know much about these things, and he was just wondering if maybe his presence was somehow putting the ghost off, when he felt something behind him. There was no sound, just an awareness that there was something there. Trying not to move too eagerly, he slowly turned and was suddenly facing the soldier, who was close enough to touch. The figure was there, right in front of him, yet somehow *not* there at the same time. He could see the soldier as clear as anything, but he could also see the trees through him. As he gazed on the soldier's face, a terrible tide of sadness swept through him, the likes of which he had not felt since the day he had seen his friend Jimmy torn to bits beside him. The soldier wore on his face a look so bereft that Alfie wanted to cry for him. Instead, he drew himself as upright as he could and looked the soldier in the eye.

"Stand down, soldier," he said. "Your job is done."

Holding his crutch tight with his armpit once again, Alfie managed to raise his hand to his forehead in a salute.

"Dismissed," he said.

He watched as the figure of the soldier became more and more substantial, and just before it disappeared completely, he was almost sure that the look on its face changed to something that was nearer a smile.

Alfie turned to head back to the house, but as he did so, he caught sight of something out of the corner of his eye, a small, dark shape with a long tail, scuttling through the grass and away.

Twenty-Four

Alfie thought he had never been quite so relieved as he was when the lorry finally came to a stop. He had been perched on the makeshift seat for so long that his buttocks were getting numb and every time the lorry hit a pothole in the road (and there seemed to be a lot of those), he had to hold tight to his crutch for fear of being pitched forwards onto the floor of the lorry. They had been driving for several hours, pausing only to drop off other discharged patients and now Alfie was the last one. Finally, he was home. It was hard to believe that it was Christmas Eve. There was no snow, no bells ringing, no decorations. While this damn war was still raging, Christmas might as well have been cancelled.

His last few hours at Calvey Manor were bittersweet. Although he was glad to be on his way home, he was sad to be leaving Helen behind. She had become a friend and a confidante and in other times and other circumstances, perhaps she could have become something more. It was a conversation they almost had the night before he left. He had gone to look for her after Doctor Shaw had told him he was to be discharged and found her outside, having a cigarette. She looked up when she heard him approach and tried to conceal the cigarette behind her back until she saw who it was.

"You caught me," she said, but the smile she gave him was so weak that he knew straight away that she had heard he was leaving.

"I won't tell," he said, then paused. "I'm leaving tomorrow," he said eventually.

"I know," she replied. "I'm pleased for you."

They looked out onto the grass and the trees. As far as Alfie knew, the ghost had not been seen since.

"Will you miss me?" he asked.

"Alfie, one way or another everyone leaves here apart from the staff. They either leave in a lorry or a box. If I missed everyone who left, I'd never stop crying."

"Sorry."

Helen took a long drag on her cigarette, then dropped the butt onto the gravel and ground it out underfoot.

"Of course I'll bloody miss you, you idiot," she said. "You weren't the worst, by any means."

Alfie reached out, placed a hand on her shoulder and drew her near.

"Maybe you could look me up when all this is over. You know where I am."

"Maybe I could," she replied. "Who knows where we'll all be by then?" She hugged him tight and then pulled back. "But you know you've got to get on with your life, Alfie, don't you? Go back to your family. They'll have missed you so much."

"I know, but I ..."

"No buts. And please don't say you love me. You won't believe how many other lads have said that and they all leave. None of this is real, Alfie. It's just...circumstances. Everything feels more extreme, but it isn't real feelings. One day it'll all be finished and then we'll see. But for now, you go home and I'll stay here."

"You gave me my life back," he said. "I'll never forget that."

"Then go and live it," Helen said. "Live it and be happy. And have a very happy Christmas with your family. Sorry there's no mistletoe."

She leaned over, kissed him quickly, then turned on her heel and went back into the house. He didn't see her again. Like Daisy, she wasn't there to see him off.

But now he was standing at the gate to the farm, and his mum and dad were hurrying down the path towards him. His mum was weeping freely and his dad looked like he was only just holding it back. He understood then that he couldn't have given them a better Christmas present if he tried.

He heard a scuffling amongst the loose stones of the wall next to the gate and a rat, with mud-matted fur squeezed out and landed on the path. Alfie was ready to aim a kick at it, but the rat sat up, looked at him with obsidian eyes, then twitched its whiskers and vanished into the long grass. Alife opened the gate and went back into his life.

The End

About the Author

Liverpool born Bob Stone is an author and bookshop owner. He has been writing for as long as he could hold a pen and some would say his handwriting has never improved. He is the author of, among other titles, two self-published children's books, *A Bushy Tale* and *A Bushy Tale: The Brush Off* and the young adult urban fantasy trilogy *Missing Beat, Beat Surrender* and Perfect Beat, all published by Beaten Track Publishing.

Bob lives in Liverpool with his wife and cat and sees no particular reason to change any of that.

By the Author

Children's Fiction

A Bushy Tale
A Bushy Tale: The Brush Off
Faith's Fairy House

Young Adult Fiction

Missing Beat
Beat Surrender
Perfect Beat

Adult Fiction

Out of Season
The Custodian of Stories
Letting the Stars Go
Check It Out Now!

Plays
Scripted: Four One-Act Plays

.

Printed in Great Britain
by Amazon

33748745R00051